I0783525

# Coffee & Cohorts

# Coffee & Cohorts

*A Dreamers Saga Short Story*

## Elizabeth Bird

ISBN:  979-8-9913364-2-0

Cover Art by Elizabeth Bird with Taylor Schoonover

First edition 2024

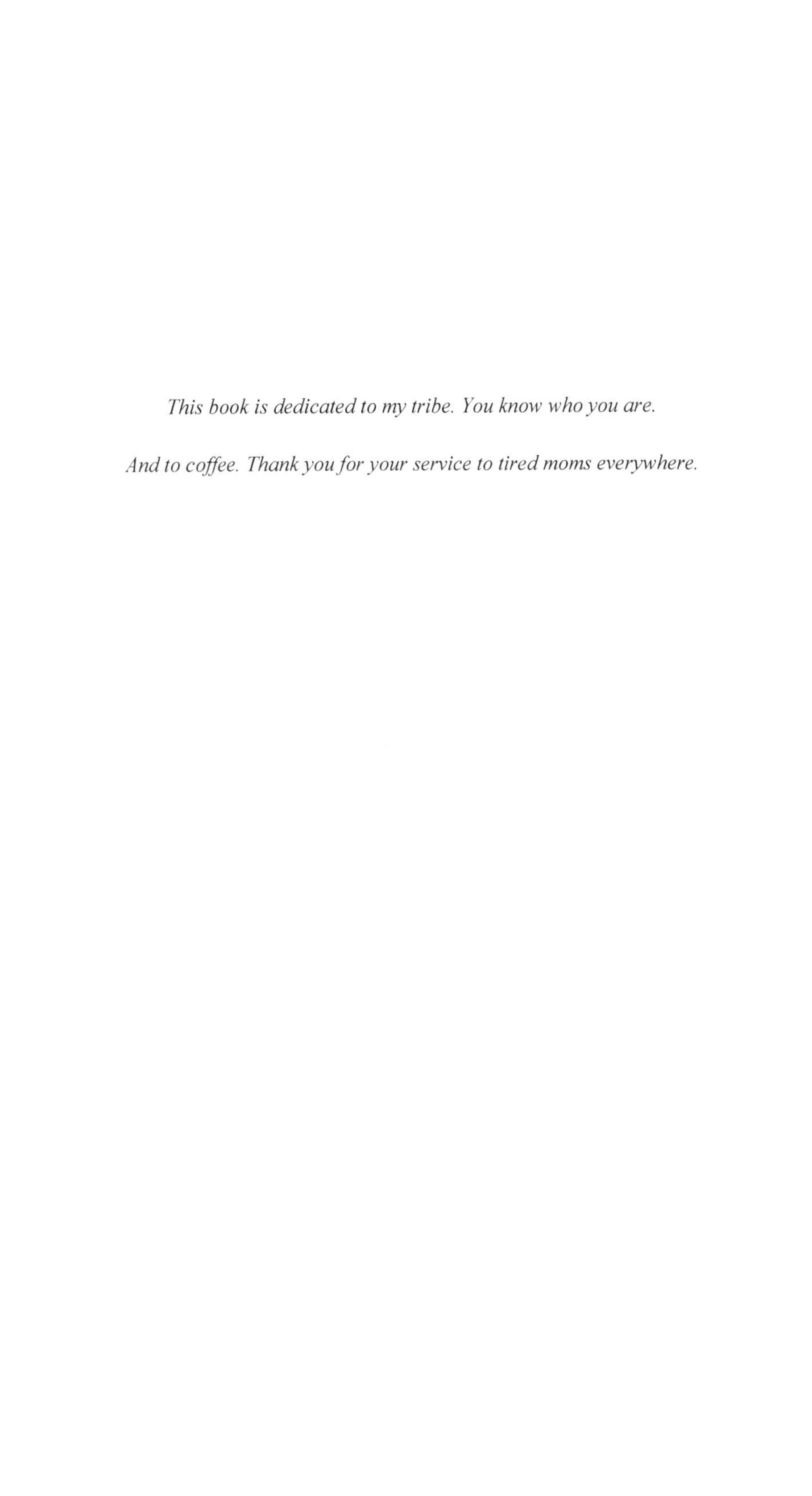

*This book is dedicated to my tribe. You know who you are.*

*And to coffee. Thank you for your service to tired moms everywhere.*

# Chapter One

# An Unexpected Introduction

It was a wonderful day.

In fact, it was shaping up to be, if not the best day ever, then at the very least somewhere in the top ten. Nessa Everette shook her chestnut hair free of whatever mess she'd tied it in hours before, sighing in relief as the coiled knot at the base of her skull finally ebbed away. Slumping down into a little café chair, she propped her poor aching feet on the table, the throbbing in her toes fading from an aching roar to a minor meow.

Nessa practically melted into a puddle then and there.

Silence. Glorious silence.

And then, she heard Maria snickering behind her.

So much for silence.

"Congrats. You made it!"

Her curvaceous co-worker spun a finger in the air to celebrate, a smirk on her red-painted lips.

"It was close." Nessa stretched her pale neck from side to side and heard it pop, her shoulders applauding in relief. "I thought I was going to have to go hide in the bakery until Ollie hosed her down."

Maria shrugged. "That's Melissa. She is large, in charge, and the biggest pain in the ass I've ever met."

Nessa snorted, putting a hand over her mouth to cover her laugh as Maria gave her a grin that could only be described as cheeky. She'd never had the pleasure of meeting Melissa I'm-Head-Of-The-Book-Club Jones until this morning, and of course it had been when the line extended out the door and

Melissa needed eleven separate orders on nine different cards and three different kinds of milk. Nessa had only been a barista at Ollie's Coffee House for about two weeks, and she had very nearly burst into tears when one of the Courtneys had changed her order from soy milk to whole milk to almond milk and then back to soy milk again.

Nessa had shotgunned the unwanted lattes rather than allow them to go to waste, which probably explained why she could see sound right now. But now that she thought about it, her senses had been playing tricks on her all afternoon. The shadows were doing strange things at the corners of her vision, wiggling and shifting in ways they shouldn't have. The depth of them didn't seem right, like they were trying, and failing, to appear darker than they needed to.

It was happening again right now. Nessa stared over Maria's shoulder, watching strange shapes form behind the espresso machine.

It was really throwing her off. Perhaps it was time to modify her caffeine intake.

Horror stories of the Syracuse Sisters Reading Society and their gloriously volatile temperaments had been relayed Nessa on the very first day of her employment at Ollie's Coffee House, and Maria had advised her that the only way to deal with urban soccer moms was to placate them with Pinot Grigio and scones until they either fell asleep, ran away, or were finally forced to go pick up their kids.

Or had to run out the door to catch their cheating husbands in the act.

Maria swore it had happened. Twice.

Nessa had attempted the scone technique until yet another Courtney had berated her for serving an iced latte cold. Bewildered, Nessa had pointed out that iced lattes contained *ice*, which was cold, and was subsequently berated for being a smartass until Ollie hurried over to personally pour them more Pinot. Maria had laughed so hard she had to go cool off in the freezer when Nessa told her what happened.

After that, she'd had the pleasure of serving the infamous Mr. Lane. He came in every day, and every single day, without fail, the menu remained a mystery to him, no matter how many times she and Maria explained how the drinks worked. Perhaps he found comfort in the ritual, or a sense of importance, but there was a time and a place for self-indulgence, and Mr. Lane didn't care if the pope himself was in the coffee line behind him. His Holiness could simply wait while he inquired about the contents of a macchiato for what had to be the hundredth time. It wasn't the line, or the crowd, that had tested Nessa to the near-breaking point.

Today had marked the fickle and unforgiving first day of freshmen enrollment at Syracuse University. Thousands of wide-eyed young students had flooded the town, along with their well-meaning-yet-overbearing-and-exhausted parents. Between the stress of campus visits, dorm tours, class selections and getting-to-know-you activities no one wanted to do, the poor newcomers had begun to resemble zombies, their heads full of nothing but names of people they'd never see again and the telephone number for student housing. Their need for caffeine had been akin to a drowning man's need for air, and the shop had been packed from the moment Ollie flipped on the Open sign.

They'd even been forced to close the shop early after running out of soy milk, oat milk, two-percent milk, almond milk, vanilla syrup, and -- most importantly -- coffee. Plus, for some strange reason, they were also out of Pinot Grigio.

*Who could have guessed*, Nessa thought, remembering the book club's rarely-empty glasses.

But none of that mattered now. Nessa's throbbing feet weren't bothering her, the ache at the base of her neck meant nothing, and the various flavored syrups on her apron and mental warfare from the book club were nothing more than a distant memory.

Because it was a *good day*.

Ollie emerged from the back office, releasing his dreads from a red handkerchief. He waved two envelopes in the air, his face creased in joy.

"Payday!"

Maria let out a *whoot!* of victory as Nessa beamed. She arched her head back, and Ollie booped her nose with the envelope.

"Don't spend it all in one place," he teased.

Nessa considered saying something snarky, but elected to keep it to herself, a knowing smile on her lips. Snatching the envelope from his hand, she was up like a shot, tossing her apron onto her designated peg by the door. The slightly-too-deep shadow against the wall practically vibrated at her approach.

But her caffeine-induced hallucinations meant nothing to her, because she was finally, *finally* free.

"See you Tuesday!" she called over her shoulder.

"Mind how you go!" Ollie replied.

Nessa inhaled deeply as the shop's bell faded behind her and marveled at the way the sky danced with vibrant color in the twilight of a New York summer, the very air tasting of heat and leaf dust. She was free for a whole day. She had nowhere to be, no classes yet, no one to answer to, and her two roommates would be gone, off getting the last of their things from home.

Best of all, she had just gotten paid, and there was a bookstore right across the street.

Nessa practically danced across the street, her sky-blue eyes alight with anticipation. Sure, her to-be-read list was longer than a country mile, but when had that ever stopped anyone? She passed the bookshop every day and had thus far resisted temptation, though the mouthwatering display of books and luscious plants in the window constantly beckoned the weary collegiate with their siren song, promising warmth and poor financial decisions. And now that she finally had some spending money, she was planning on a nice little treat for herself…or maybe half a dozen.

She opened the door to Literary Greens with a little flourish, gazing around in excitement. The shop was no bigger than the coffee house and stuffed to the brim with charm, with mismatched Edison-bulb lights hanging haphazardly from the ceiling and black and white tile floors gleaming between rows upon rows of books.

Nessa wasn't certain if the walls were painted dark green or if they just appeared green because of all the plants. Lush vines hung from the ceiling beams, ferns and bushes nestled around the tables, and even several trees rested in large pots on the floor. Green of every shade poked out between even more greenery and the various rainbow hues of succulent spines.

Nessa couldn't stop her smile as she ran her fingers reverently along a row of books, the smooth covers under her hand settling her overstrained nerves as the air wrapped her in the familiar smells of ink and paper mixed with dust and greenery. It smelled like reading in her backyard after school, or the many nights around the fire on the patio, her father spinning tales of old like a master. She wanted the smell of this place bottled into a perfume so she could take it everywhere.

Her eyes traveled down the titles in the row in front of her, noticing some she'd never seen before and others that greeted her like old friends.

Oh, she was going to like it here.

"I will be right with you!"

The cool, delicate voice had come from somewhere amongst the foliage, and Nessa found herself drifting further into the leaves, her head tilting as something in her chest warmed and swirled, like a hot coffee on a rainy day. Her fingers found the pendant at the base of her throat, a clear, deep blue stone set in swirls of silver. It warmed at her touch, and immediately a sense of comfort wrapped around her.

Out of the corner of her eye, she saw a shadow lengthen across the floor.

Nessa quickly snapped her head around to see…nothing. Only a dark plant leaf bobbing up and down.

She stared at it suspiciously. Nessa had tried to get along with plants; she *wanted* to get along with plants, but all her attempts thus far had ended in failure and death. She had managed to keep one lone ficus alive, though she wasn't certain if that meant her skills were improving or if the ficus was simply the Chuck Norris of the plant world.

Instead of lingering on her thoughts, she reached for a book. It was smaller, and paperback, because spending less per book meant getting to buy more books. And more books meant a happier Nessa.

A sudden crash made her jump a mile high, and she looked behind her to see a young woman standing in the middle of the store, a shattered pot at her feet. She was striking like a newly sharpened knife (or maybe that was just the sharpness of her cheekbones), her long, white-blonde braid draped over one slender shoulder. There was a depth to her beauty that reminded Nessa of the ocean, gorgeous on the surface with untold mysteries underneath.

At the moment, her delicately sharp features were set in an expression of absolute shock, her green eyes wide as she gawked at Nessa.

"Are you okay?" Nessa asked.

The other girl blinked, shaking herself from her stupor.

"Yes, I…I…will just get a broom, and…"

She glided off with all the strength and grace of a ballerina, and Nessa watched with a furrowed brow.

How could someone possibly move that smoothly?

"Are you sure you're okay?"

"Oh, yes. Yes, I am fine!" the woman called from the back.

Well, that was a lie. Nessa knew frazzled when she saw it. Heck, she'd had plenty of experience with it today. Too many first-time parents sending their precious baby off to college, the copious amounts of caffeine doing nothing to settle their shattered nerves.

Nessa's own were still doing funny things, courtesy of her multiple lattes. The shadows outside the shop were wiggling again.

She replaced the book on the shelf and knelt carefully to gather up the shattered pottery, sympathy for a fellow service worker igniting her desire to help. Or maybe it was something else. She'd barely spoken two words to the other girl, but Nessa already knew she *liked* her. Something in her voice and her movement felt reassuring, like a memory from a favorite dream.

Luckily, the plant didn't appear any worse for wear, and she gently brushed her fingers over the green and white leaves. They felt soft and almost waxy. Nessa couldn't tell much else, other than the fact that the plant appeared strikingly healthy.

*What a lucky little thing*, she mused. *Aside from getting dropped…*

"You do not have to do that."

Nessa glanced up to see the young woman hiding among the leaves, her pale skin glowing even paler against the shadowy green. Those captivating eyes roiled with something Nessa couldn't quite place.

"I don't mind. Accidents happen." She dropped the pottery shards into the wastebin. "Are you sure you're okay?"

"I am fine." The other girl gave Nessa a small smile as she fully emerged from the greenery. "I am just new and don't want to find out what my boss will say once he hears I dropped a plant."

"I hear you," Nessa said with a small laugh. "I just started at Ollie's across the street. I dropped a full mug on my second day and nearly burst into tears."

"Too nervous?"

"Too hot." Nessa rolled her eyes at herself. "I should have known better. I'm only just starting to get feeling back in my fingertips."

"My fingers appear to have a different problem. I cannot hold on to things, apparently."

The young woman knelt to the ground and carefully scooped up the plant as if it were her own child, the tension melting from her face as she assessed her little charge. She placed it reverently in a new pot, carefully packing the soil with the calm serenity of a priestess at worship. Nessa couldn't help but watch in awe.

"Could you hold this part up for me?" the other girl asked Nessa, carefully holding back some leaves.

Nessa nodded, dropping to her knees and placing her hand where the young woman's had been a second before as the other girl patted the soil around the plant. Nessa could have sworn she heard the plant sigh in relief.

She stood once she'd finished, wiping her dirt-covered hands on a green apron sporting the shop's logo. "Can I help you find something?"

"What?" Nessa blinked, shaking herself out of her stupor. "Oh, no. I'm just looking for a new book." A pause. "Or *books*."

The young lady almost laughed, and Nessa felt her cheeks burn crimson. Her mild obsession with the written word had opened her up to more than a few jabs in her life. It wasn't possible to bring two books a day to school without people noticing.

Middle school girls could be so vicious.

The need to apologize overwhelmed her. "I work across the street, so I'm sorry, but you'll probably be seeing a lot of me."

"I would not mind that," the other girl replied. "You seem nice. I just moved here and do not really know anyone yet."

Nessa held out a hand. "I'm Nessa."

The young woman took it, her grip firm. "Livia. Livia Aeris."

"Nice to meet you, Livia."

And it was. It *really* was.

"Well now, Nessa," Livia leaned conspiratorially on her broom handle, her green eyes shimmering with mischief, "what do you like to read?"

Nessa felt a slow, wicked grin cross her lips. "What have you got?"

The next two hours passed in a blur of chatter and book titles, the conversation flowing as naturally as breathing. To Nessa, it felt as though they were picking up an old conversation they had never finished. Nessa revealed her love of fantasy and magical worlds, while Livia demonstrated her complete disinterest in sci-fi, claiming it made her head hurt too much.

As Nessa gradually filled her arms with books, Livia bustled about, taking immaculate care of the shop's plants. She knew seemingly everything about every single one: their leaves, bloom-times, how much sunlight and water they needed, and even different soil types. She said she'd been gardening since she was a child.

"I was raised to treat all things that grow with reverence, and I found myself rather good at it."

"I killed a cactus once," Nessa admitted, the corners of her lips turning downward. "I forgot to water it. Then, when I finally did remember, I overwatered it, and then… Well, it clearly wanted to die. It was a mercy killing, honestly. It was never the same after my neighbor's cat got into it."

Livia looked at her with a mixture of concern and horror.

"I was six!" Nessa defended herself. "A cactus is clearly too much responsibility for a six-year-old. I blame my parents, really."

Liv pointed the plant mister at her and Nessa suddenly realized a cheap plastic bottle could be incredibly threatening.

"Stay away from my plants."

"Yes, ma'am."

"Liv is fine."

"Yes, Liv."

Liv nodded, apparently satisfied. "Did you find anything you like? I hate to cut this short, but I need to close up soon."

"Oh! Yeah!"

Nessa had nearly forgotten about the pile of books she'd amassed at the front counter, which said something about her conversation with Liv. They'd known each other for barely two hours, but already there was a familiarity to their conversation, to Liv's presence. It felt like Nessa had known something like this long ago, a kind of nostalgia for something she didn't even remember. But whatever it was, she had missed it.

She glanced out the front window and realized the sun had set. Streetlights were flickering on as twilight settled into a gentle summer's night. Well, most of the streetlights, anyway. The one in front of Ollie's sputtered, then went out with a *pop*.

Strange. The campus maintenance had replaced the bulb just yesterday. She remembered because she hadn't been paying attention and had walked under the ladder instead of around it, only noticing when Maria, who was superstitious, had doused her with holy water before she'd even crossed the threshold. Luckily, Nessa's book hadn't been harmed.

Maybe they hadn't screwed the bulb in right? The darkness in front of Ollie's appeared to deepen, and she frowned. It wasn't *that* dark outside. She could still make out the silhouettes of the trees along the rest of the street, along with the shops and even the occasional person hurrying by. But the darkness in front of the coffee shop was different. It appeared endless, as if something was absorbing all the light, and the edges of the shadows were doing odd things, wiggling like heat lines off a tarmac.

Nessa played with her pendant, shaking her head as she attempted to get her thoughts in order.

"What is it?" Liv asked.

"Nothing." Nessa forced a smile. "Just some weird vibes, is all."

"Do you get those a lot?" Liv's tone hinted at a deeper question Nessa didn't quite understand.

"Sometimes, but not often." She shrugged, eyeing Liv warily. "You're not one of those New Age Aquarians, are you?"

Liv blinked. "I have no idea what that is."

"Then you're definitely not a New Age Aquarian."

"…Is that a good thing?" Liv arched a perfectly precise brow, and Nessa found herself impressed with her skill.

"If you were, your life would probably be more interesting," Nessa admitted. "But also more complicated. Those astrological charts get messy pretty quickly."

Liv laughed a little. "This was fun. I am glad you came in."

"I am too." Nessa carefully began placing her new books in her backpack.

"Would you possibly want to do this again?" Liv eyed Nessa with a look she couldn't place. "You could give me some recommendations for more titles to order for the store."

"Yes!" Nessa practically bounced on her heels. "I can stop by before my shift on Tuesday."

"Perfect." Liv beamed. "I will see you on Tuesday."

Nessa left Literary Greens with a heavier bag and a lightness in her step, unable to help the stupid grin plastered on her pretty face. She'd been paid, she had new books and time to read them, and most importantly, she might just have made a new friend.

She had enrolled early at Syracuse University with the help of her adoptive father, a prominent literature professor from Berkley, but a consequence of early enrollment was that she had moved to campus before any of the other students. She'd spent the past month in an empty dorm on an empty campus full of empty classrooms, and that had been her life up until today: work, an empty room, and a microwave mac and cheese. Rinse and repeat.

She didn't want to admit it, but the last few weeks had been horribly lonely.

Nessa had left her family and all her friends back in San Francisco when she'd come to Syracuse. She could have gone to Berkley with her father, but she wanted this, she wanted an *adventure*, and while getting transported to Panem or King's Landing or even Wonderland sounded like a terrible idea, starting fresh in a place where she had the freedom to recreate herself felt like exactly what she needed.

And it *was*, but no one had ever mentioned how lonely it would be, or how isolating.

She hadn't felt any of that when she'd been talking with Liv, however. Nessa's adoptive mother, Lilly, had said the key to college was finding your tribe. Find the people who understand and care about you, and you'll be fine, Lilly had told her.

Lilly had found her own tribe in a sorority, while her future husband had founded a reading club that had quickly devolved into a drinking club, and the friends they'd made there had been crazy aunts and uncles to Nessa growing up. She was only just starting to build her tribe, and she'd already decided Liv was going to be part of it.

Nessa turned to make her way down the street, musing happily over her new tribemate and debating which book she should start first. Normally, she would start a batch of cookies when she got home, but student housing didn't allow things like ovens. Too many drunken escapades involving burnt toast and a three a.m. fire drill, no doubt.

She was lost in her happy thoughts when suddenly, and without warning, the streetlight above her flickered out.

# Chapter Two

# Lights Out

Nessa glanced up at the bulb as she adjusted her backpack. The fixture hummed, the light returning once before flickering again. Goosebumps rose on her arms along with the hair at the back of her neck, and she swallowed down the tightness in her throat, a feeling of foreboding tingling down her spine.

She let out a long breath to settle her stomach. What did she know, anyway? The streetlights were old; she'd seen campus maintenance fiddling with them all week. Something must be wrong with the wiring.

Right, that was it. The wiring.

Her fingers flew to her pendant as her back went ramrod straight to the point of pain, the muscles in her jaw coiling down tight and refusing to release. She clutched at the necklace, the metal and crystal warm against her skin.

Something was *wrong*.

Nessa glanced frantically down the street toward the coffee shop. The rest of the street remained illuminated; she could see the darkened windows of Ollie's and Literary Greens, the subpar landscaping the city barely cared to maintain, and the empty sidewalk just fine.

A sound like a long, hissing exhale sent shivers down her spine as she suddenly felt eyes on the back of her neck, and she sensed more than saw something reaching out for her.

She froze for a moment, then spun to find herself alone on the street. Her eyes searched through the pockets of light and the shadows in between, but there was nothing. Not a soul and not a sound. No wind. No buzzing of the streetlamps.

Silent as the grave.

Nessa forced her body to move. She felt it again, unseen eyes following her into the safety of the light, and she shuddered, swallowing down shallow gasps of air as her eyes scanned the street again. Though the night was mild, she shivered, a repulsive creeping feeling racing over her skin.

Where was this coming from?

She tightened her grip on her bag. *Think. Think. Think!* Someone had to be out here with her; she could *feel* it in the air. It was the same sense that whispered that you weren't alone in the house. And had it gotten colder? She tried to listen for footsteps, but could hear only the pounding in her ears.

Nessa had felt this way only a handful of times in her life, usually when she was in a crowded place. At those times, she could feel *someone's* eyes on her, but those eyes always felt different. They felt secure, like a parent watching over a child.

This wasn't protectiveness. This was malice.

This was a hunter watching prey.

There was a loud buzzing sound followed by a *POP*, and Nessa nearly jumped out of her skin, spinning back toward the coffee shop. The streetlight at the end of the block exploded into sparks, sending the corner of the street into absolute darkness. It wasn't so much an absence of light as an absorption of it. Nothing could escape.

Her muscles wound tight under her skin, rattling her very bones, and Nessa swallowed hard, forcing her body to remain perfectly still. Moving would catch the attention of whoever…or *whatever* was out here with her.

The loud buzz behind her was the only warning she received before the light at the opposite corner shattered in a rain of sparks.

That. Wasn't. Normal.

Nessa wanted to move, but she couldn't decide on a direction. She broke into a cold sweat, tasting fear sour on her tongue. All those lattes in her stomach suddenly felt like a very bad idea.

It came again from her other side, a buzz and a pop before another light was claimed by darkness. Then, back on her left, another buzz and pop, and another light went out.

The light above her began to flicker, strobing on and off so rapidly she couldn't keep track. There was no longer any safe pool of light.

Only the encroaching darkness.

It happened again, *buzz* and *pop!* Then from behind her, *buzz* and *pop!* Now in front, *buzz* and *pop!* Like dominoes falling, the lights exploded one by one.

All converging on her.

Nessa bolted back to Literary Greens. Panicking, she grabbed for the door, but her sweaty hands slipped on the handle. She scrabbled at the entrance, her heartbeat rocking her frame, but the door refused to budge as she pounded on the wood in desperation. *In! In! In!* The darkness was only three lights away, then two.

Then one.

It was coming.

The light above her began to buzz, and Nessa's wide eyes flew up, watching the bulb blaze brighter and brighter before she dove to the side, seeing stars behind her closed eyes when she hit the ground. She shivered madly as the bulb shattered, barely missing the cowering girl with a rain of glass and sparks. Covering her head, she swallowed a cry and held her breath, squeezing her eyes tightly closed.

She lay frozen, hardly daring to breathe, but nothing else happened.

Nessa opened her eyes and then wasn't sure she actually had. There was only darkness, sitting heavy on her chest and temples and making her head pound as she struggled for air. Shapes danced in the dark, writhing like liquid oil slicks, and she held perfectly still, closing her eyes against the images.

Holding her breath, she waited.

Slowly, the oppressive feeling faded. With each thundering beat of her heart, she felt the pressure ebbing away, like water draining from a leaky dam. She didn't feel watched anymore. The eyes had moved on.

Nessa sat up, searching the darkened street, and saw only everyday shadows. Brushing herself off, she carefully pushed herself to her feet, clenching her fists to ease the trembling in her hands. Her lungs loosened as she gulped down air, letting out a shaky breath.

"What the hell?"

It had to be a fluke. The power had probably surged and blown out the streetlights. Yeah, that was it, an unexpected power surge. And the sensation of being watched? That could have been the street cameras, or a stray cat, or something else mundane. She was just causing herself to freak out; it was all nothing more than the power of suggestion.

Right. Suggestion.

At the very least, there definitely wasn't a creature lurking in the darkness, hellbent on terrorizing her. Obviously, it couldn't be that.

…Right?

She had nearly managed to convince herself when suddenly, from behind her, she heard the sound of shattering glass.

# Chapter Three

# Shadow Man

Nessa whirled, her backpack falling to the ground with a *thunk* as she frantically scanned the silent street. The shop windows were dark, the only light coming from the distant stars, and it would have been picturesque if not for the shattered glass littering the sidewalks. And the dark shadow that surrounded Ollie's Coffee House.

The large glass window at the front of the shop was gone. Cautiously, Nessa approached the building, shivering as she crossed into that horrible darkness, her air coming in silent, shallow gasps. Swallowing did nothing to wash away the acrid taste of sandpaper and cotton balls in her mouth, but she did her best to choke down her fear along with not enough spit.

This was a terrible, no good, very bad idea; her heart and her mind were in complete agreement on that. She knew better than to move towards the scary sound. She knew how to *not* be the damsel in the first five minutes of a horror movie.

But this wasn't just some random shop, this was *her* shop. And she wasn't about to let some burglar or ghost or whatever it was scare her away.

Ollie's was *hers*, and she would fight to the last to protect it.

The gaping hole was large enough for the weekly delivery truck to pass through, and Nessa hardly recognized the shop that only hours earlier had been warm and inviting. Now, it sat dark, empty, and cold, the glass littering the tile floor sparkling menacingly in the dim light. Her eyes found the silhouettes of the tables and chairs, exactly as she and Maria had left them.

The shadows of the chair arms and table legs turned sharp in the lack of light as the darkness crawled across the tile floor, seeming to reach out for her. The coffee counter along the far wall appeared undisturbed, and the warning bell above the door remained silent, the homey shop looking like a mockery of itself in the dark.

Nessa carefully climbed over the broken glass into the shop, hearing the shards crunching beneath her shoes. The minute noise sounded almost discordant against the gloom as the too-thick air pressed against her temples, the room growing so cold she could see her shuddering breaths creating phantoms in the dark.

This wasn't right; Ollie's was a home, *her* home. It was meant to smell of vanilla and cinnamon and coffee, not of cold and snow and darkness. The shop was safe. It was supposed to be *safe...*

The darkness pressed against her chest, and she attempted to take a deep breath to fight the constriction in her lungs, only to lose the struggle. Her shaking palms grew damp with sweat, and she tried to dry them on her shorts but found her shoulders and back wound down too tight. She couldn't move.

Why would anyone break in, if they'd apparently left the register alone? Was some poor co-ed drunk? Maybe it had been a prank, or a dare? Her wide eyes fell to her shoes, and she saw thick pieces of glass embedded in the soles, nearly ripping through to her skin. She froze in her tracks as she suddenly realized what was missing.

*Why is there no blood?*

The shards on the floor glinted, looking sharp and easily large enough to cut. Yet she could find no blood droplets on the floor, and the larger pieces were cracking under even her minor weight. So why were all the pieces still so big; how had the intruder managed to not cut themselves or step on them?

*Unless...*

Nessa's hand flew to her pendant, her fingers following the silver swirls. This was a bad idea. She should go. She should run out of here now, and...

Her apron was gone.

Nessa's heart leapt into her throat, cutting off all her air. She'd left the apron on the hook by the door, she *knew* she had.

Now it was gone. Her wild eyes stared at the empty peg.

The apron...

*Her* apron.

A *thud* rang out from the back, and she flung herself backward with a gasp, wincing as something sharp sliced into her palm. She swallowed a cry at the sight of the blood oozing from the cut and watched as it dripped slowly to the floor, the darkness turning the liquid from red to black.

*"Viiiiisssssseeeeriillllll...Viiiiissssssseeeeriillllll..."*

That hadn't been the breeze.

Something was coming.

The hair on her neck and arms shot straight up, her stomach churning as her nerve finally broke. She skidded on the broken glass, scrambling as she frantically launched herself over the counter, and huddled by the spare syrups. Pulling her knees in close to her body, she held her bleeding hand to her chest.

Help, she needed *help*.

Her shaking hands fumbled for the shop's phone, and she cursed herself for being stupid enough to drop her bag – along with her phone -- outside.

*"Viiiiisssssseeeeriilllll…Viiiiisssssseeeeriilllll…"*

The line made no noise. It was dead. She hadn't even known a landline could go dead.

Porcelain shattered as the darkness crept in around her, and she put a hand over her mouth to quiet her erratic breathing. She could hear it coming now; chairs squeaked across the floor, thumping into walls and tables as something skittered across the tiles, making a quiet *tap-tap-tap* sound.

The exit light blinked out.

Nessa stared at the back of house and prayed to any god that would listen for help as her spine threatened to shake her apart, cold sweat dripping into her burning eyes. It did nothing to ease the sense of dread in her chest.

*"Viiiiisssssseeeeriilllll…Viiiiisssssseeeeriilllll…"*

The whispers grew closer. A soft *click-click-click* sound that might have been claws on tile surrounded the counter, and Nessa bit her tongue until she tasted blood. *Don't move.*

*Don't. Move.*

The end of the coffee shop suddenly collapsed into absolute black. This wasn't darkness. This was *nothingness*. No shapes, no light, nothing could escape…

And it had been following her.

Nessa swallowed a scream.

The black abyss shuddered, rippling with iridescence as it coalesced suddenly into the shape of a man. No, not a man, a man-shaped *thing*. The shoulders didn't look right, nor did the knees. And the *face*…

The shadow man passed into a beam of moonlight, and she saw that it had no eyes -- only the barest impression where eyes should have been, above what looked like the idea of a nose and a slim mouth.

A mouth filled with rows and rows of teeth.

*"Viiiiisssssseeeeriilllll…Viiiiisssssseeeeriilllll…"*

Nessa swallowed down her sickness, blinking back hot tears as cold crept up her arms and legs and her very muscles tingled like static. She ordered her body to move, but it refused, so she sat shivering, frozen in choking terror.

She squeezed her eyes closed, not wanting to watch what the shadow man would do to her. She couldn't. She had to think of something else, something besides her paralyzing fear. If she did the courageous thing, courage would come.

She hoped.

Grinding her teeth, Nessa thought of her new friend Liv, of Ollie and Maria, of her parents Lilly and Albert. She thought of the horror stories her adoptive father told around the fire on warm summer nights, nights she desperately missed. Of old friends and staying up late to watch favorite shows where handsome men fought monsters.

Wait…that was it!

Using the last of her courage, Nessa grabbed a saltshaker and chucked it into the darkness, the shadow man flinching as the little glass jar was absorbed into the black. The projectile hit the floor with a small *clink*.

That was all she needed.

Grabbing a second saltshaker, then a third and a fourth, she chucked them wildly at the terrifying thing, at the darkness itself seemingly made flesh. It stumbled back with every hit, a low hiss coming from somewhere other than its mouth, and she scrambled up, launching herself over the counter. She crashed to the ground, seeing stars when her shoulder slammed against the floor.

*Get out! Out! OUT!*

"What the…"

Nessa didn't get a chance to finish as the shadow man rose slowly from behind the counter.

Instead, she cursed.

Spectacularly.

# Chapter Four

# Escape

She slid back along the floor on her rear in her mad struggle to get away, the shadow man appearing to grow taller and taller until the abyssal darkness nearly enveloped the whole shop. The creature skittered over the counter, the placement of each hand and foot somehow a threat, and the entire shop rattled with the movement, pots, pans, bottles and china all crashing to the floor. The shadow man held its head high, looking like it was…sniffing?

*"Viiiiissssssseeeeriillllll…Viiiiisssssseeeeriilllll…"*

The barest idea of words drifted in the chilly air, and Nessa's body shuddered against them. She ground her teeth, forcing herself to stand up as she swallowed down bile along with her terror.

*Focus! Think!*

It was sniffing the air and tilting its head side to side.

It couldn't see.

Carefully, Nessa picked up a shard of glass from under her feet, keeping her breathing shallow and silent as she watched it search. The shadow man's head spun, tasting the air and listening.

She threw the shard as hard as she could, the glass shattering against the bakery door, and the head of the man-like thing swiveled toward the clatter. Nessa held her breath, waiting.

It turned, skittering off to the back of the shop and melting away into the darkness. She waited a beat, then two, as the shadows around her lessened in intensity.

Silently, she released a shaky breath, nearly swaying with the force of her heart crashing against her ribs. Her hand on the counter steadied her as her knees nearly buckled under her weight, and the shop spun around her for a moment before she collapsed. Why were her temples pounding so hard?

What *was* that? What kind of man carried darkness with him like a shield?

…She wasn't even sure if it had *been* a man.

Nessa shook her head firmly. No. She couldn't think about that now. She had to get out of here, and *quietly*.

She turned to the window. It would certainly be the fastest way out, but there was no way to avoid the glass scattered along the floor. The path to the door was clear, but then she would have the shop's bell, two locks and the doorknob to worry about. The burglar, or whoever he was, would certainly hear that. At least with the window, she could always launch herself out if he returned suddenly.

Nessa carefully pushed herself up and took an uncertain step around the edge of the scattered glass. Then a second.

Suddenly, the shop was plunged back into cold darkness, and she stumbled against the wall in terror. In a sudden *whoosh*, the shadow man was on her, leaning over her and hissing.

*"Viiiiisssssssseeeeriillllll."*

Nessa squeezed her eyes shut, her hands covering her mouth as her eyes burned with unshed tears of terror. She shivered, pinpricks of cold burying into her bones, and tried to breathe, but found her lungs couldn't expand.

The shadow man leaned down, sniffing her hair as Nessa swallowed a scream. *Don't look.*

She didn't want to watch, she didn't want to see what he was going to do to her.

*"Viiiiissssssseeeeriillllll…Viiiiisssssss-"*

A loud *CLANG!* echoed through the shop, and the darkness snapped back into honest shadows as the man (the thing?) collapsed to the floor.

Standing in the middle of the ruined shop, iron frying pan raised, was Liv. She looked like a triumphant shieldmaiden of old, a bright beam of light in the darkness.

Nessa blinked at her in shock.

"Are you okay?" Liv asked, looking concerned. She reached for Nessa, and Nessa nearly collapsed into Liv's arms.

"Whoa! Whoa! It's okay. I've got you."

"Uh…yeah. Yeah, I'm fine…"

It was a lie.

Liv quickly turned her away from the crumpled shape on the floor. "Come on. You are coming to my place, and we can call whoever we need to call."

"Okay." Nessa nodded. "I'm good now. I'm good."

Liv didn't let go of her until they were standing on the sidewalk before Literary Greens, the warm night air chasing away the chill in her bones and forcing the last traces of terror from her heart.

"What the hell *was* that?" Nessa rolled her sore shoulder.

"I do not know." Worry crept into Liv's voice as she bowed over the shop's lock. She didn't look at Nessa.

Nessa stared at her, wide-eyed. "You're *lying*."

She wasn't sure how she knew, but she did. It was the subtle shift in tone, the clarity of Liv's eyes, the mild concern where fear should be.

Liv knew who the shadow man was.

"They should not be here." Liv shook her head. "I do not know why they are."

"Who?"

"It does not matter. No one should be breaking into your coffee shop, Nessa."

"No one…oh, hell!" Nessa swore. The shop! Someone had to call Ollie, or the police, or both; there was an unconscious burglar on the floor!

"Are you okay?" Liv asked her.

"Cut myself on some glass, but I'll be fine," Nessa admitted as Liv took hold of her bleeding hand.

"Let's get you cleaned up, then."

# Chapter Five

# One Sided

Ollie beat the police there by five minutes, while Liv brewed Nessa some smelly tea to settle her nerves. Nessa hadn't even asked what was in it. Honestly, she didn't really care; she'd do whatever it took to stop shaking.

The burglar had disappeared by the time the police arrived on the scene, but they said the chances of him coming back were small. Most thieves knew better than to return to the scene of the crime. All the same, the Syracuse police department promised to station a cruiser outside the shop for the next couple nights to keep an eye on everything, especially now that it would be completely dark. No one had an explanation for the streetlights.

With a large glow-in-the-dark bandage on her arm and a boatload of tea in her stomach, Nessa was able to recount to Ollie and the assembled officers what had happened, though she left out the feeling of the darkness creeping in on her. That had probably been her imagination, just her mind playing tricks. It had only been a simple break-in, and she'd gotten spooked.

Even so, the image of the shadow man refused to leave her.

No. She had simply scared herself.

…Right?

Ollie said the cashbox was intact, which meant that life, though not great, was for the moment at least manageable. He credited Nessa with scaring off the burglar, and therefore saving his business.

"Why don't you take an extra day off? You've been through enough, I think." Ollie gave Nessa a little side hug.

Nessa shook her head. "I'm not going to let this make me afraid of the shop. I like working here too much. You and Maria are awesome."

"Said the college girl who just chased off a burglar for me." Ollie patted her shoulder. "Really, if you need to take some time, it's okay."

"I'm fine." Nessa shook him off. "I'm a little spooked, is all, but I'm a brave girl, Ollie. I kill my own spiders and everything."

"Okay. But don't stay alone tonight. You got anywhere you can go?"

Liv spoke up suddenly. "She's staying with me. I'll keep an eye on her."

Nessa gave Liv an epic dose of side-eye. Sure, they liked each other, but they had only met today. Why would Liv stick her neck out like that? For her? Then again, they had just fought off a burglar together, which she was given to understand constituted a bonding experience.

At least it'd been a man of flesh and blood, not a mountain troll.

"Yeah," Nessa agreed reluctantly. "I'm with Liv tonight. I'll be okay."

And somehow, she knew she would be.

After statements had been made and the window boarded up, Liv guided Nessa back to Literary Greens and into the back room. In most businesses, the back room would be reserved for office supplies and barely used Christmas decorations, but here it held boxes and boxes of unopened books, and hundreds if not thousands of plants. Liv even brushed her fingers against some as she passed by.

They stepped through a door at the other end of the room, and Liv led Nessa up a short winding staircase and through another door. When Liv flicked on the light, Nessa was greeted with a small, nearly empty apartment.

The living room was nothing more than carpet and white walls covered in greenery, and the only thing more numerous than the plants were the piles and piles of books. Most were paperbacks with broken spines and dog-eared covers, tucked between sparse furniture that looked like it had been there for at least thirty years.

The living room opened onto a kitchenette that was far from flashy, but immaculately kept, and in the opposite direction was a hallway with three doors. Liv's bedroom and a bathroom, probably.

"It is not much," Liv said, sounding almost shy, "but it is home."

Nessa turned to face her. "Why are you doing this for me?"

"I like you, and I want to help." Liv shut and locked the door behind them as Nessa pretended not to notice. "Besides, it is my fault you were out so late. I feel a little responsible."

"Well, don't," Nessa told her. "I've done stupider stuff in my life."

"Really?"

"…No." She sighed and ran a hand through her hair, then pointed to the kitchen. "May I?"

"Help yourself."

Nessa scoured the kitchen and found the basics: flour, eggs, butter, bananas…oh, and chocolate chips. There wasn't any brown sugar, but honey worked just as well as molasses…

Everything was here. She could make cookies.

A flicker of joy and normalcy ignited in her chest, and she couldn't help the loony grin that spread across her face as she inhaled, smelling green plants and hot tea and eucalyptus.

Everything was going to be okay.

"What are you doing?" Liv asked as she put the kettle on.

"Making cookies." Nessa caught an egg before it rolled off the counter. "Baking helps me think."

"Tea does the same for me."

"What was that thing, Liv?" Nessa cracked the eggs into the bowl with one hand, frowning at the incomplete batter. "That shadow man?"

Liv shrugged. "I only saw a burglar. It was probably just a desperate person looking for money. People can do crazy things with proper motivation."

Nessa head bobbed in reluctant agreement. How many of the true crime podcasts she listened to had said that very thing? But…

She'd been raised in San Francisco and her upbringing had exposed her to a wide range of colorful human beings, but she'd never seen anything like *that*. And there was something niggling at the back of her brain.

"Still…"

"Yes?"

"It didn't…*feel* right." Nessa poured too many -- and yet still not enough -- chocolate chips into the dough.

"I cannot imagine a burglary ever feels right."

"I guess." Nessa shrugged, conceding in the face of Liv's unyielding logic. "Thanks for coming to get me."

"Anytime."

"Maybe I should start carrying around a frying pan for self-defense."

Liv pursed her lips. "I do believe the campus police would notice."

…She was probably right. Darn Liv and her logic.

Nessa didn't want to admit it, but she was glad that after the cookies were consumed and it was time for bed that she wasn't alone. Burglar or no, she really didn't want to be alone tonight, not after everything she'd seen and felt at the coffee shop. She knew sleep wouldn't come easy. Not tonight.

Which was how Nessa found herself staring at the construction-grade popcorn ceiling of Liv's guest room at nearly one in the morning. She was sprawled on sheets that smelled of eucalyptus and fresh air, thinking so loudly she was surprised Liv couldn't hear her all the way down the hall.

It had only been a burglar. It had only been an ordinary man, but men were scary enough. Was that why she felt so unsettled?

Then, she heard it. A loud *thump*.

From downstairs.

Nessa was up like a shot. She sat perfectly still, listening.

*Thump. Thump. Thump.*

Flinging off the covers, she raced for the door, only to meet Liv in the hallway.

"Did you—"

"Yes." Liv smiled. "It was me. I just came up from the store."

Nessa sighed in relief.

"I thought…"

Liv's tone turned frigid. "It is taken care of."

"The burglar didn't…"

"I took care of my shop. That is all."

The flash of stormy anger behind Liv's eyes caused a pit to open in Nessa's stomach. Somehow, she knew better than to inquire further.

# Epilogue

# Cinnamon Roll Queen

Wednesday dawned sunny, clear and hot, and as Nessa entered Ollie's Coffee House she was greeted by Ollie, Maria, and a Syracuse Securities technician, who was cheerfully installing a new security system and trying to convince Ollie to buy more cameras. She inhaled deeply, her shoulders relaxing instantly as the smell of fresh coffee, vanilla and cinnamon washed over her.

Home was home once more.

"*Moooorningggg!*" Maria sang, much too cheerfully for someone who had been awake since dawn. "I made you a reward for defeating the creeper!"

Nessa rolled her eyes. "I didn't defeat anything." She went to reach for her apron, only to find an empty peg.

*Oh, right.* Her stomach clenched.

After she restarted her heart, she grabbed Ollie's instead. He never wore it anyway.

Maria waved a hand airily. "You still saved my job, and for that, I'm feeding you."

With little flourish, she placed a still-warm cinnamon roll the size of Nessa's head on the table in front of her.

The noise that came from Nessa's mouth was wildly inappropriate for baked goods.

Ollie looked up from his conversation with the technician, likely desperate to change the subject from thermal sensors and why he needed them immediately. "Hey kiddo, when's your birthday, anyway?"

"Uh…" Nessa quickly swallowed down her bite of cinnamon roll. Sweetness washed over her tongue, and she tasted just a touch of nutmeg. She nearly collapsed to the floor in bliss, but forced herself to answer her boss's question.

"November fifth. Why?" She shoved another bite of pastry in her mouth as soon as the words were out.

Nessa actually wasn't certain of her true birthday, but November fifth was the day her parents had adopted her. Since they'd never found her birth certificate, the Everettes had decided it was as good a day as any to celebrate their child's birth.

"I think the security code should be associated with my shop's protector."

Nessa swallowed another decadent mouthful of cinnamon roll. "I hid behind the counter. Hardly the stuff of legends."

"Too late," Maria giggled, knighting Nessa with two karate chops to the shoulder. "You are now the Dame of Ollie's Coffee House, Protector of the Caffeinated Realm."

Nessa's snicker was cut off by the happy chiming of the shop's bell, and Livia Aeris stepped through the door.

"Good morning, Liv." Nessa licked the frosting from her fingers, fighting the urge to lick the plate clean.

Because she was an *adult*.

After spending two solid days and nights together, Nessa was surprised to see the other girl. She'd thought Liv would surely be sick of her by now.

Instead, Liv smiled at her. "Hello, Nessa. Am I interrupting?"

"I was just dubbed Queen of the Cinnamon Rolls."

Liv's face broke into a wide grin, a look Nessa couldn't place alighting in those expressive green eyes. With a flourish, she flared out her skirt, dropping into a deep and practiced curtsy.

"Your Highness," she offered.

Nessa rolled her eyes. "Oh, shut up."

Surrounded by the laughter of her friends, Nessa opened up the shop for another busy day.

# Chapter One

# Never Trust A Good Cosplay

*Remain calm.* Nessa had to remember this was something she had prepared for. She could do this.

Nessa Everette had realized a long time ago that she had very little control over her own life. One could only do so much. For all the planning in the world, something unexpected was always bound to happen. She tried not to let those things get to her. Worrying only meant you suffered twice, after all. No amount of anxiety could change the weather, nor would it prevent a history professor from deciding to be cruel during finals week. She knew this from many canceled picnics and several vindictive history enthusiasts. There was simply no controlling the other people in her life.

She could, however, control her own facial expression when speaking to Mr. Lane.

"What is a 'caramel latte?'" The elderly man leaned over the counter to see the menu better, his bushy eyebrows knitting together as he adjusted his glasses. Nessa's smile tightened when she heard Maria snicker behind her. Of course, Maria had good reason to feel self-satisfied. She was usually the one who had to wait on the infamous Mr. Lane, but today Nessa had somehow gotten roped into it.

She was less than thrilled. If she tightened her smile any more, her lips were bound to split. *Just keep smiling. Get a tip. Buy more books.* Buying food probably wouldn't be a bad idea, either.

There were forty-three different drinks on the menu of Ollie's Coffee House, ranging from drip coffee to smoothies to milkshakes masquerading as coffee, and in the last fifteen minutes, Mr. Lane had inquired about the contents of thirty-

1

seven of them. This was a daily ritual. None of this information was new to Mr. Lane. And yet, he still managed to look pensive and uncertain about his choices, day after day.

Why hadn't Nessa hidden in the bakery when she'd had the chance? Oh, that's right. Melissa I'm-Head-Of-The-Book-Club Jones just *had* to order eleven separate drinks. She also had eleven separate cards to run and of course Lydia had to change her order twice. All this drudgery had stranded poor Nessa at the register when Mr. Lane made his appearance.

Everyone had a breaking point. Nessa was almost at hers.

"It's steamed milk with espresso and caramel flavoring, Mr. Lane." Nessa's forced cheerfulness made Maria's head pop up like a meerkat. She could see the other barista's reaction in her peripheral vision. Maria, and Ollie for that matter, had come to know that tone of voice. Nessa was only able to produce it when she smiled so hard her lips couldn't move and her jaw ground her teeth together.

She was nearly finished with a double shift that had included both the Sunday brunch *and* lunch crowd. She'd had a frat boy drop a chair on her foot, a child fling syrup on her apron and whipped cream squirted in her face by a high school girl who didn't know how cream-in-a-can worked, all before noon. Then there was the local book club, currently heading into hour three of sulking in their usual corner. They were like children, in that they cried or screamed when they wanted attention or were bored.

Maria and Ollie shared a look. Ollie pursed his lips and nodded — and then, distracted by his silent exchange with Maria, managed to pour scalding hot coffee directly into the lap of Melissa I'm-Head-Of-The-Book-Club Jones. She shrieked, and Ollie began apologizing profusely.

Nessa wasn't quite sure what Melissa's middle name was. It might actually have been Jones, since she introduced herself every week as, 'Melissa Jones, I'm head of the book club.' Nessa, being a halfway intelligent girl, did not need the reminder.

The bell over the door chimed happily, and Nessa let out a soft puff of air to reset her smile into something more natural and less murderous. Bells were *good* things. Their happy little chiming meant the arrival of someone — or, depending on what religion and superstitions one belonged to, some*thing*. Nessa liked the bell over the coffee shop door because it normally meant a person she liked was here. Most frequently it was her best friend, Liv. But today had been such a whirlwind that Nessa had stopped taking notice of the tinkling bell. It had been hours since the shop was quiet enough to hear it.

She glanced at the door and froze solid.

Who in the Blessed name was that?

Nessa's blue eyes widened as her jaw went slack, all feigned friendliness forgotten. A young man towered in the doorway to the shop, casting a long, threatening shadow across the floor. His appearance alone was enough to silence the entirety of the book club. All eleven of the suburban housewives were gawking open-mouthed at him.

The menacing young man looked back at the glass door, smiling slightly from under uneven dark scruff. He looked like he was trying to grow a long beard, but hadn't fully hit puberty yet. His eyes traveled up to the bell, and he gave it a playful flick before turning to survey the coffee shop with sharp eyes and an amused smirk. He had to be at least Nessa's age, or maybe slightly older, with darkly tanned skin and faint wrinkles around his eyes. The boy could have been one of those hipster types, complete with man bun and beard oil, but that description didn't quite fit. For one thing, there wasn't a scrap of flannel in sight; instead, he was decked out in leathers and furs. The strange look was completed with tunic, boots, and an air of misplacement.

A glint of silver caught Nessa's eye. Was he wearing a sword? Yep, that was a sword, alright. Who wore a sword to a coffee shop? There was no way that thing could be real. The campus police would have tackled him to the ground the instant he so much as breathed in their direction. Then again, Nessa's faith in the generally overweight and out of shape campus law enforcement was only slightly stronger than her belief that she would pass her Calculus midterm. Was there a Renaissance fair in town, or some sort of Game of Thrones reenactment happening? She shook her head, attempting to clear the muddled thoughts from her brain.

Her stomach clenched as she shuffled her feet slightly, her back going ramrod straight. When had she started clutching the edge of the counter? She forced her fingers to relax and felt the muscles in her wrists strain from tension. Why couldn't she get a full breath? Air was suddenly coming to her in quick, shallow gasps; none of it would stay in her lungs. The already soft lights of the store seemed to dim even further as Nessa ripped her eyes away from the strange boy.

*Don't stare*, she told herself.

"Isn't he odd?" Mr. Lane grumbled from the other side of the counter. Nessa didn't hear him.

Syracuse was a college town, so she shouldn't be surprised by a little oddness. College was a time to experiment, and some people experimented differently, so strange things happened all the time.

Then why? Why had a thrill of fear settled in her stomach? He was only some whack job who dressed funny. She had survived Shark Week with frat boys who thought they were God's gift to women, even avoided crazy religious zealots preaching about how she was going to hell for getting an education as a female. Both kinds of troublemakers had been forcibly removed from campus. This boy hadn't even opened his mouth yet; he couldn't mean them any harm…could he?

That sword at his hip looked like evidence to the contrary.

Her fingers flew to the pendant at the base of her throat. Something was off. The air in the coffee shop had changed from friendly to foreboding with his arrival. How could one boy silence an entire room just by walking in?

A shiver ran down her spine.

"…Hmmm?" She jumped, realizing suddenly that Maria had been speaking. Blinking a few times to clear the cobwebs from her mind, she shuffled a little too clumsily over to Maria. The other girl was staring at her.

"I said, Ness…" Maria put a gentle hand on her arm, the gesture snapping Nessa back to Earth. Maria raised two perfectly sculpted brows at Nessa, a slight smile on her red-painted lips, and moved her attention to Mr. Lane. The older man's response was to roll his eyes and Maria's smile flashed briefly to a sneer. She snapped back to Nessa, the sweet smile returning. "Ollie needs you. I'll finish checking out Mr. Lane."

"Sure." Nessa's jaw unclenched, and she nodded. She moved along the back counter toward the door, the pads of her fingers skimming along the cold stone counter. She felt as though there was some memory just out of her reach. Something was stuck in her mind that she should remember…she should…

She shook her head once and everything fell into place with a snap. She had to focus on work. Get paid, buy food, pay tuition, become a famous author and literature professor. She was so busy focusing that she nearly ran straight into Ollie's chest.

Ollie reached out to steady her and Nessa reflexively grabbed his muscular arm, blinking up at him in surprise. The world came back into focus for the second time in five minutes. She *had* to get it together.

"You alright, kid?" Ollie lowered his head to get a better look at her face. Nessa wasn't exactly short, but Ollie was close to seven feet tall; *everyone* was short compared to him. "Your whole back went rigid as soon Jon Snow hit the door."

"Yeah, he threw me, is all."

Nessa was making an effort to not even look at the wild boy, much less notice that he was prowling around the perimeter of the shop like a caged animal, his eyes scanning the room. The pads of her fingers skimmed over the smooth surface of the clear, deep blue stone at her throat, following the intricate silver swirls of the setting. Her breath started to come slower and deeper the moment she felt the cool crystal and silver metal under her palm.

They both turned to see the book club still staring at the strange boy. She had *never* seen those women silent before, let alone for any length of time. Perhaps there was a silver lining to this weirdness after all.

"I'll kick him out if he tries anything, okay?" Ollie pulled the rainbow bandana from his head, his massive pile of dreads falling loose, and wiped it down his face. He let out a long breath.

"I know, Ollie." Nessa gave her boss a brave smile. With Ollie's past as both bartender and doorman, she had no doubt of his ability to enforce the threat. It wouldn't be the first time Ollie'd had to 'help' someone out of the shop for harassing her or Maria, usually for the safety of the poor, misguided Neanderthals. Maria had been known to slap a few customers with wandering hands, and while Nessa had considered the idea herself, she was generally far too timid.

Today, however, might be a good day to reconsider.

She chanced a glance over at the dark, wild boy and found his eyes flitting between her and Maria at the register. Every time Maria caught him looking, her scowl deepened. His eyes landed on Nessa again and she took a step closer to Ollie, who put a hand on her shoulder and angled her away from the boy's gaze, staring down the scruffy Jon Snow look-a-like on behalf of his skittish waitress. Nessa swallowed hard.

"Something wicked this way comes," she muttered under her breath.

The bell over the door rang again. Nessa turned a little too quickly, her heart already running away in her chest. A young woman with flowing white-blonde hair stepped through the door, her bright green eyes scanning the shop before they settled on Nessa. Nessa felt the tension in her shoulders melt the instant her blue eyes met green, and she smiled. Livia Aeris smiled back, giving a little finger waggle of a wave to her best friend.

Nessa took a deep breath for the first time since the strange boy had entered the shop.

Backup had arrived.

"Did you know Liv was coming in when you said that?" Ollie quirked a brow at her, trying — and failing — to hide his smile.

"No." Nessa's bow-shaped lips stretched into an amused smile of her own. "But she's got the best timing."

She took the coffee pot from Ollie and went to fix Liv her usual, watching out of the corner of her eye as the oddly dressed mountain man took a seat directly in the middle of the room. Liv placed herself in her usual spot in the back corner, settling herself near the counter Nessa currently occupied so Nessa could stop to chat in between running orders. This seat also allowed Liv see the entire shop. Nessa had noticed that Liv seemed to have a problem sitting with her back to a door, but she was never sure if this was a conscious decision on Liv's part or not.

"Ness?" Maria had come over, and Nessa turned her sky-blue eyes to the curvaceous other woman. "What do you think of Legolas over there?"

Nessa's pretty pink lips twitched. "Legolas was the elf, Maria. He's more Boromir than Legolas."

"Didn't Boromir die?" Maria asked, leaning her luscious backside on the counter beside Nessa.

Nessa nodded and blew a piece of chestnut hair from her eyes, trying to focus on the movement of her hands and not the eyes she could feel drilling into her back. Hot water, tea leaves, splash of lemon…where was the giant green mug?

"Yep," she replied, popping the end of the word with her lips. She glanced over her shoulder again, unable to help herself. She didn't like taking her eyes off the strange man for long. Something about him made her skin crawl.

Had she ever seen him before? No, of course not. The only burly mountain man she was interested in was Strider, and he was fictional. She pinched her lower lip between her teeth to bring herself back to reality. She had to focus on work, not on carefully crafted fantasy sagas.

Maria arched a dark brow at her. "Think he'll hit on you?"

Nessa snorted. She knew she was cute at best. Both Liv and Maria were prettier than she was. Liv was tall and long and Maria was a perfect hourglass, while Nessa was somewhere in-between, falling more on the boyish side. She felt nothing about her was particularly distinctive except for her blue eyes. Liv had an elegant face with high cheekbones and snowy skin, while Maria's copper skin glowed in the sun like a jewel. Nessa wasn't curvy and exotic like Maria, nor tall and elegant like Liv. She thought she was just … sweet.

"Not with you in the room." Nessa nudged Maria playfully with her hip.

Maria's red lips parted in a wicked grin. "Jon Snow isn't exactly my type."

Nessa rolled her eyes as she took the coffee pot and Liv's usual giant mug of tea out to the front of the counter, stopping by Liv first to postpone meeting the wild boy for as long as possible. Liv stretched her long legs out in front of her and crossed her feet at the ankles, an expression of forced calm on her beautiful face.

"Hello, Nessa." She smiled up at her friend.

Nessa smiled back as she set Liv's tea in front of her. "Hey Liv." She felt her shoulders relax a little further.

Liv glanced around Nessa at the scruffy boy, a perfectly groomed blonde brow arching toward her hairline. No one could arch a brow like Livia Aeris. In fact, Nessa was certain her current expression could make whole armies think twice before invading. There was a sharpness under Liv's sympathetic air that let you know she was not a woman to cross. Now, she settled back in her seat with both hands wrapped around her mug, her face a calm sea: beautiful and serene with a fierce riptide just below the surface.

"When did he appear?" Liv's cool voice tinkled like silver bells. She took a delicate sip of her tea.

"About sixty seconds before you came in." Nessa shrugged, refusing to look back at the boy. She could feel him staring at her, though, his eyes burning a hole in her neck. Her fingers flew to her pendant again.

She told herself to be a big girl and just get it over with. Liv was here. Liv always had her back. She glanced toward the back counter, where Maria and Ollie were standing side by side, arms crossed and glaring at the boy.

"I'll be right back," she told Liv, plastering a forced smile on her face as she approached the Jon Snow doppelganger.

He looked up at her and the air stuck in her lungs. She had read plenty of novels where something like this happened, a stranger entering someone's perfectly normal life. No good ever came of it.

"Can I help you?" Nessa's years of waitressing took over. *Smile, be polite, earn tips to pay for books.*

"I'm looking for someone," he answered in a strange, thick accent Nessa couldn't place. It wasn't German or French but sounded like a mix between the two, some lilt of western European. Obviously, he wasn't from Syracuse, or even New York. Nessa herself was from San Francisco and people still claimed she had an accent. This was a vicious lie, of course; everyone here sounded like they were from New York while she spoke normally.

"You look lost." She set the empty mug in front of him and began to fill it, keeping her eyes firmly on her work instead of him. She had chosen one of the smaller mugs on purpose, hoping that once he was finished with his drink, he would leave. "And fair warning, pick-up lines like that don't work on me."

"What?" He blinked up at her. "Pick-up lines?"

"Flirting." Nessa nodded to Liv in the corner. "My friend over there is a master of mental warfare, and she's protective."

Liv's green eyes were burning into the pair. When she saw them looking over at her, she smirked with a joy that didn't reach her eyes and gave another little finger-wiggle wave. Her fingers could have been mistaken for dancing blades, her expression a thinly veiled threat. The ferocity of the angry sea was barely being kept in check.

"I see." He looked back up at Nessa. "I'm looking for a girl."

"Men usually are," Nessa almost snapped.

Good Lord, was he another creeper? Chances were high; men like that came in all the time. They would order coffee, make small talk, and then try to do what they called flirting, and what Nessa called borderline assault. Though that happened less and less the more Liv was around. And anyway, what sane man walked around carrying a sword?

He narrowed his eyes. "A girl named Nessa."

Nessa nearly dropped the coffee pot.

Fear settled in her belly, her teeth clamping down on her lower lip to keep her gasp inside her chest. *Don't look at him. Just don't*, she thought frantically. Some sixth sense was telling her it would be a bad idea. Her hands trembled. and she clenched them around the coffee pot till they hurt. She glanced over at Liv, who had straightened in her chair, her mouth a grim line. Her friend's gaze had turned cold and calculating. She looked ready to pounce.

Nessa swallowed hard, forcing herself to breathe. The boy's scrutiny had turned to Liv in the corner, and Nessa was pretty sure the entire coffee shop could feel the murderous vibe radiating from her usually serene friend.

"...Why?" She willed herself to appear calm, arching a brow at the boy as he turned back to her.

He grinned up at her. "Only to speak with her about her family."

Nessa swallowed down a squeak along with her lunch. Her family? What about them? This strange boy couldn't possibly know her, or her parents. Cold fingers ran down her spine and she clamped her mouth shut to keep the bile down. Her parents were teachers. Lilly and Albert Everette had adopted her before she was even two years old. They had lived a very simple and loving life in San Francisco. There was nothing to talk about.

*Could he mean…?*

No. Not even her adoptive parents knew who her biological parents were, though it certainly wasn't for lack of trying. But no matter how hard they'd looked, nothing was ever found. Three private investigators later, not one single clue had turned up. They couldn't even find Nessa's original birth certificate.

So how could this wild boy possibly know anything about them? That had to be what he was implying, right? Or was he threatening her? Trying to bait her? This had to be some sort of scheme. What did he want? Money?

Heat flashed through her stomach and her vision. She may have only been nineteen, but Nessa was no fool. She set the coffee pot down on the table with more force than necessary and straightened to her admittedly unimpressive full height.

Liv's attention immediately snapped to Nessa. The boy's response was to quirk his lips in a way that made Nessa's stomach drop into her toes. She turned to look at Maria, who nodded.

Great. She had backup.

"Why don't you enlighten me?" Nessa gritted through clenched teeth. "Then I can tell you if she would even *want* to speak to you."

"I'm afraid it is a private matter."

He leaned toward her and her heart jumped into her throat at the definitely-not-threatening posture. Seeing this, he grinned cruelly. "...Your Highness."

The words made Nessa's chest freeze. She swallowed, pointing to the door. "Then I'm afraid you must get out of my shop."

*Your Highness?* What kind of psycho crap was that?

The boy leaned back in his chair as though it were a sunny day at the beach, that wickedly smug expression still on his face. He looked her up and down.

"That's a lovely pendant you have..."

"I said, get out!" She raised her voice but kept it firm, hoping he wouldn't notice her hands trembling.

Liv leaned forward in her chair as Ollie suddenly appeared next to Nessa. Ollie might have been lean, but he was still more intimidating than Nessa's relatively petite five-foot-six frame. He crossed his arms over his chest and took a step forward so Nessa was half behind him.

Snow looked over at him, both eyebrows shooting up.

"Is there a problem here?" Ollie more stated than asked.

A dark grin appeared on the boy's face, his eyes sparkling with something that made Nessa's skin crawl. How could a man manage to look pleased and malicious at the same time?

The strange boy rose, turned away, then paused and turned back to Nessa.

"My lady." He gave a low bow, his eyes lingering on the terrified waitress. Then he turned on his heel and left the coffee shop.

Nessa didn't take a breath until the door closed behind him.

She swallowed hard, feeling like she was going to collapse into a puddle on the floor right then and there, when Liv, tea in hand, materialized at Nessa's side along with Maria. Her friend's hand found its way to her shoulder, the mug of tea appearing like magic in front of her. Nessa took it with trembling fingers as Maria let out a low whistle, voicing what they were all thinking.

"That is one crazed-up fruit loop."

# About the Author

Elizabeth Bird is a Kansas City born fantasy author. She began writing at thirteen, but admittedly didn't get good at it until her late twenties. Her love of stories grew with the arrival of her two daughters, which she blames on her darling husband. She has collected a host of skills like teaching and acting to make story time awesome for her kids. She is proud to say that after over 20 years in the making, *The Azure Crown* is her debut novel.

Follow her social media @elizabethbirdwrites or go to her website at www.elizabethbirdwrites.com